PUFFIN BOO

STRANGER DANGER?

Anne Fine was born and educated in the
Midlands, and now lives in County Durham.
She has written numerous highly acclaimed and
prize-winning books for children and adults.

Her novel *Goggle-Eyes* won the *Guardian*
Children's Fiction Award and the Carnegie Medal,
and was adapted for television by the BBC; *Flour
Babies* won the Carnegie Medal and the
Whitbread Children's Novel Award; *Bill's New
Frock* won a Smarties Award; *Madame Doubtfire*
has become a major feature film by Twentieth
Century Fox starring Robin Williams, and, most
recently, *The Tulip Touch* was the winner of the
Whitbread Children's Book of the Year Award
for 1996.

Anne Fine
Stranger Danger?

Illustrated by Strawberrie Donnelly

PUFFIN BOOKS

PUFFIN BOOKS

Published by the Penguin Group
Penguin Books Ltd, 80 Strand, London WC2R 0RL, England
Penguin Group (USA), Inc., 375 Hudson Street, New York, New York 10014, USA
Penguin Books Australia Ltd, 250 Camberwell Road, Camberwell, Victoria 3124, Australia
Penguin Books Canada Ltd, 10 Alcorn Avenue, Toronto, Ontario, Canada M4V 3B2
Penguin Books India (P) Ltd, 11 Community Centre, Panchsheel Park, New Delhi – 110 017, India
Penguin Group (NZ), cnr Airborne and Rosedale Roads, Albany, Auckland 1310, New Zealand
Penguin Books (South Africa) (Pty) Ltd, 24 Sturdee Avenue, Rosebank 2196, South Africa

Penguin Books Ltd, Registered Offices: 80 Strand, London WC2R 0RL, England

www.penguin.com

First published by Hamish Hamilton 1989
Published in Puffin Books 1991
Published in this edition 2000
7 9 10 8 6

Text copyright © Anne Fine, 1989
Illustrations copyright © Strawberrie Donnelly, 2000
All rights reserved

The moral right of the author and illustrator has been asserted

Printed in China by Midas Printing Ltd

British Library Cataloguing in Publication Data
A CIP catalogue record for this book is available from the British Library

ISBN 13: 978-0-14130-913-2
ISBN 10: 0-141-30913-X

··· Chapter One ···

On Monday morning a policeman came to Joe's class to show everybody a film and give them a talk.

The film was called *Stranger Danger*. Joe didn't see much of it. He was under the table, trying to coax a baby daddy-long-legs on to the palm of his hand. He heard a bit of the film, though. He heard, *Never take sweets from a stranger,* and, *Never go with a stranger.* Joe thought the baby daddy-long-legs must have seen the same film. It wouldn't put even one step on Joe's hand, and Joe didn't like to pick it up in case one of its legs fell off.

Afterwards, the policeman spoke to everybody. He was good fun, and made a lot of jokes. Mostly he talked about being careful.

"Don't worry about being *too* careful," he said. "You *can't* be too careful. You have to use your common sense. Now, let's hear from everybody. What is the first safety rule?"

"Never take sweets from a

stranger!" everyone chanted.

"Right!" said the policeman. "And
that means food and drink and
anything at all that goes in your
mouth."

He paused, and stuck his thumb
in his mouth like a baby. Everyone
giggled.

He took his thumb out and looked serious again.

"And what is the other safety rule?" he asked.

"Never go with a stranger," everyone chanted.

"I can't hear you," he said, cupping his ears and looking puzzled.

"*Never go with a stranger!*" everyone shouted.

"I still can't hear," he said.

"You'll have to speak up. I must be going a bit deaf."

"NEVER GO WITH A STRANGER," everyone bellowed.

"That's good," he said. "Now don't forget!"

And winking goodbye at Joe's teacher, Mrs Murray, he settled his helmet back on his head, and went off.

Joe looked down at the floor again, but, frightened by the noise, his baby daddy-long-legs had disappeared.

··· Chapter Two ···

Later, the classroom door swung open and in walked a lady Joe had never seen before. Steel spectacles hung on a chain around her neck, and in her hand she was carrying a list.

"Eye tests," she said, and nodded at Mrs Murray, who was busy in the reading corner.

Mrs Murray nodded back.

The lady put on her spectacles and looked down her list. Joe hoped it wasn't in alphabetical order. He always came first.

"Arnold," she said. "Joe Arnold. Is he here?"

Joe put his head down and kept quiet.

Mrs Murray looked up from the reading corner and said, "Off you go, Joe."

Joe stared. The lady was a perfect stranger! Maybe she'd nodded across the room to Mrs Murray, but Joe had never seen her before in his life. And *Stranger Danger*. Hadn't the policeman only just finished showing them the film?

The lady was beginning to look just a little bit impatient. She tapped her list.

"Where are you, Joe?" she said. "Out you come."

Joe scraped his feet against the legs of his table, but he didn't stand up.

"Hurry up, Joe," said Mrs Murray. "It's only an eye test. You just look at pictures and colours, and answer questions about what you see. Then we know if you need to wear glasses."

Still Joe didn't move. He sat fiddling with the pencils on his desk.

"Go along, Joe," said Mrs Murray. "Now!"

She sounded as if she meant it.

So Joe scraped back his chair
and followed the lady out of the
room. All the way down the
corridor he was furious. He was
angry with the lady, but he was
even more angry with Mrs Murray.
What was the point of inviting a
policeman into the class to warn
everybody *Never go with a stranger*
when the first thing you did was get
cross with someone who tried to do
as they had been
told?

He dragged his feet, falling even
further behind.

The lady turned round.

"What *is* the matter with you,
Joe?" she asked. "Are you nervous?
Eye tests don't hurt."

Joe wanted to explain. "*Stranger
Danger!*" he wanted to say. "I'm

just trying to do what the policeman said." But, then again, the policeman also said you had to use your common sense. And they were still in the school corridor, with lots of people about. And if he yelled, they'd all come running straight away to see what was the matter. And the lady knew Mrs Murray, and Mrs Murray knew her. And Joe had taken a note home about the eye tests. And the lady did have a real alphabetical list with his full name right at the top.

"All right," he said. And he walked faster, to catch up.

The eye test was fun. He sat in the chair, and she held a torch with a tiny bright light that danced on his eyeballs. She gave him a long tube like a telescope to look through, and held up odd shapes and fancy patterns that jumped before his eyes. Then she hung up a chart with some really silly pictures. There was a fish mending his socks under water, and an octopus pushing four prams at once. He enjoyed the eye test a lot, and was sorry when it finished.

"There," said the lady. "That wasn't so bad, was it?"

Joe grinned.

The lady studied her list. "When you get back to your classroom," she said, "tell Simeon Barnes to run along and see me, will you?"

"Right," said Joe. And when he got back, he told Simeon he was next on the list.

Simeon just rushed off straight away.

··· Chapter Three ···

After school Joe ran home. It was a special evening. Joe's brother Tom had got his first important job playing the violin in a big orchestra, and all the family had tickets for the concert even though it was miles away, in Easthampton.

Nana was waiting at the door,

all dressed up in a new flowery suit.
Joe rushed upstairs. His mother was
crouched in front of the mirror in
his bedroom, wearing her fanciest
dress and putting on lipstick.

Joe looked at the clothes she'd
laid out for him on the bed. Last
year's smart trousers which were
too tight now; his new white shirt
that was too big still; old-fashioned
shiny black shoes that used to
belong to his brother; and the red
tie he hated.

"I can't wear this lot."

Joe's mother smacked her
lipsticky lips, and turned around.

"Joe," she said. "It's a very
special evening. You think you'll
look silly in these clothes, but when

you get to the concert hall, you'll
see you look like everybody else."

Joe didn't believe her, but he
didn't bother to argue. Nobody ever
won a battle with Mum when she
was all dressed up and wearing
lipstick.

Grandpa and Joe's father were
waiting by the car. They were in
dark suits and white shirts, too.

Even the car had been through the car wash. It was, Joe realized, a very special evening indeed.

It was a long journey. If anyone had asked Joe what he'd done in school, he might have told them about the policeman and the baby daddy-long-legs, and *Stranger Danger* and the safety rules. But they were all too busy talking about Tom and his violin, so in the end Joe fell asleep.

He only woke after they reached the concert hall. Joe stood with his grandparents on the wide marble steps, waiting for his parents to come back from parking the car. When they appeared, the two of them were strolling arm in arm, not looking like themselves at all, more like two smart and elegant guests in someone else's wedding photographs.

Then everyone walked up the marble steps into the concert hall. It was enormous. It was *massive*. You could have driven buses between the pillars in the corridors, and that was just around the edges.

Inside, it was even more astonishing – rows and rows of

seats, hundreds of rows, more than you could have imagined in one building. His whole school could have sat in just two rows. You'd practically need a rocket to get to the ceiling. You could run half-mile races round the edge.

Each seat was covered with red velvet. Great chandeliers hung overhead. Thick drapes held back with golden ropes hung at each doorway,

and there were fifty doorways at least. People were <u>milling</u> through them, and everyone was dressed smartly. A lot of the men wore fancy bow-ties. Some of the ladies' dresses brushed the floor.

"See?" Joe's mother said, squeezing his arm. "It's a *very* special evening."

Joe gazed up at the platform, filled with empty chairs and music stands.

"What about Tom?" he asked. "Where will he sit?"

"Towards the back," said Grandpa. "Third violins. It might be just a little difficult to see him."

A little difficult? It was impossible! When all the men and

women of the orchestra had filed in, and bowed, and sat down to play the first piece of music, all Joe could see of his brother was the point of his bow shooting up and down with all the other third violins at the back.

His mother didn't seem to mind, though. She sat on the very edge of her red velvet seat, and stared over the sea of grey curly perms and bald heads as if Tom were sitting right at the front.

And his father didn't seem to
mind, either. He leaned back in his
seat and closed his eyes, and smiled
as the music floated over him.

Nana also had her eyes closed.
But she wasn't smiling as the music
floated over her. She was asleep.
The seats were soft and

comfortable, and it had been a long drive.

Grandpa wasn't asleep, but he wasn't listening to the music either. He'd switched his hearing-aid off. Joe watched him peeping furtively towards Nana to check that she was really asleep; then, stealthily, he slid the little plastic control box out of his pocket, and flicked the tiny lever from ON to OFF.

Joe couldn't blame him. The music was pretty boring. All swoopings and swirlings of violins, which was probably why his brother Tom was so keen on it. It didn't seem to *go* anywhere. It just went on and on and on. Joe settled down for a really boring time.

And then he felt a
tickle in his throat.

Cough!

Joe looked round,
panicking.

Cough, cough!

The tickle was worse.

Cough, cough, cough, cough!

The man in front shifted irritably
in his seat. The noise was bothering
him, you could tell.

Cough, cough, cough, *cough*!

The lady on Joe's left was
glowering at him now. He wondered
if he ought to squeeze
past her, and all the
other people between
himself and the
gangway, and leave

the concert hall. But when he glanced round, all he could see was the long, long walk up the aisle to the doorway, and thousands of people who would stare at him.

Cough, *cough,* cough, *cough*!

His cheeks were <u>fiery</u> with embarrassment. In his ears, his coughing sounded louder than the music. He longed to crouch down in his seat, roll up and disappear – *anything.* His cough was ruining this very special evening.

Suddenly he felt a tap on his shoulder. Oh, no! Someone had had enough!

25

Terrified, he twisted in his seat
and turned to face whoever was
going to complain. But he was
wrong. It wasn't a scowling face at
all. It was a white-haired gentleman
who was leaning forward and
offering him a peppermint to suck.

Gratefully Joe reached out – then

remembered the other safety rule:

Never take sweets from a stranger.
He drew his hand back smartly, as if
he'd been scorched, and shook his
head. He thought the old gentleman
might be irritated with him for
changing his mind at the last
moment. But he just shrugged and
looked sorry for Joe, as if he
understood why he couldn't take one.

But sorry doesn't help.

Cough, *cough, cough, cough*!

Joe was in misery. He turned to
his parents, but Mum was still
gazing enraptured towards the
orchestra, and Dad was still leaning
back with his eyes closed. How
could he ask if it was all right to
take a peppermint? He couldn't

reach far enough to jog Dad's elbow. He couldn't whisper to Grandpa to do it because the hearing-aid was switched off. And if he woke Nana suddenly, she'd shoot upright and yell, "*What?*" very loudly. She always did. It came from living with Grandpa who was always switching off his hearing-aid.

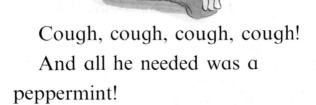

Cough, cough, cough, cough! And all he needed was a peppermint!

Cough, *cough*!

"You have to use your common sense," the policeman had said. Joe thought about it. Here he was, safe in a huge concert hall filled with people. The old gentleman offered him the peppermint because he couldn't stop coughing. He wasn't trying to poison him. And if Joe only could have asked, he knew his mother would have smiled her thanks at the old gentleman, and let him take it.

Joe swivelled in his seat and gave the man a pleading look. Luckily he understood at once, and leaning forward in his seat, he offered the peppermints again.

Joe took one and popped it in his mouth. The cough stopped at once.

The man in front stopped shifting in his seat. The lady on his left stopped glowering. Even the music began to sound soothing. Joe felt so relieved, he almost found himself enjoying the swooping, swirling violins.

Minutes passed, but the cough never returned to bother him. He spent the time pleasantly enough. He counted bald heads bobbing up and down in front of him. And then grey perms. But, mostly, he just sat listening to the music and thinking of the lady who swept him off for

the eye test and the old gentleman
who gave him the peppermint.

Most strangers are probably
good people, Joe thought. And it's
nice to be friendly. If someone you've
never seen before says, "New bike?"

to you on the pavement, you like to be able to tell them, "Yes, it's my birthday present." And when you're patting a puppy outside a shop and then the owner comes out and says, "It's all right. He won't bite", it's nice to ask, "How old is he?" or "What's his name?" You don't just shrug and set your face and walk away. You try to be pleasant.

But you have to stay safe, too. That's why they make you learn the safety rules – so you will always stop and think, and always use your common sense.

Then, while Joe was still thinking about it, the violins seemed to gather themselves up for the very last time, and with a tremendous drum roll and a clash of cymbals,

the music finished. Nana shot upright and yelled *"What?"* but no one heard her over the outburst of applause. Seeing hands clapping all around him, Grandpa furtively slid his hand in his pocket to switch his hearing-aid back from OFF to ON.

And when the orchestra stood up to take a bow, Joe even saw his brother Tom lift his head quicker than any of the others, and give a quick wink over their bent backs.

The concert was over.

··· Chapter Four ···

After the clapping ended, the orchestra filed off the stage, and everyone in the hall began to shuffle towards the doorways, politely saying, "Excuse me" and "I beg your pardon" as they trampled on one another's toes.

Joe's father glanced at Nana,

whose eyelids were still droopy from sleep.

"You stay here while we fetch the car," he said.

"Stay close to Nana and Grandpa, Joe," Mum warned. "Don't disappear in the crowd."

They hurried ahead to the car park while Nana and Grandpa took their time, waiting for the crush to thin a little before they tried to get through the doorway. Outside, the

marble steps were wet, and there were puddles everywhere. People were vanishing into the darkness.

Joe stood beneath an archway and watched as Nana and Grandpa helped one another slowly and carefully down the first few steps.

Suddenly a man slipped through the archway beside Joe. He wore a musician's dark suit and white bow tie, and he was carrying a black case, taller and fatter than himself,

and shaped like a vast overgrown
violin. Joe knew enough about an
orchestra to guess there was a
double bass inside. He watched with
interest. Maybe this man was a
friend of his brother's.

Just as the man hurried by, Joe
heard a sudden *snap*. The lock on
the double bass case had broken.

Almost at once, the wide stiff front began to swing open.

Hastily the man threw his arms around it to push it shut. Then he rested the case on the ground and thought for a moment. Joe saw the problem straight away. If the man started down the marble steps, the lid would swing open again. His double bass might tumble out, and clatter down the steps and be ruined.

The man was frowning now. He looked at his watch. Then he glanced up and saw Joe standing, watching.

The man's face cleared.

"Hello there!" he called out in a friendly way. "Could you give me a little bit of help here? Can you help me carry this down to the car park?"

Joe glanced down the steps. Nana and Grandpa were almost at the bottom now. They would be turning to look for him in a moment.

He could say yes. The man had asked for help. And he was in the orchestra. And he might even be a friend of Tom's . . .

But Joe could say no, too. And though there were still lots of people on the steps, he wasn't so sure about bits of the car park. He ought to stay close to Nana and Grandpa. It might seem mean, or even rude. But there was the safety rule, after all. *Never go with a stranger.*

Joe shook his head and started

down the steps.

"I'm sorry," he called back. "I have to stay close."

And without waiting to hear whether the man replied or not, he scampered towards Nana and Grandpa as fast as possible.

Grandpa was holding Nana by the arm, and peering at headlights, trying to see if the right car was coming.

Joe took his hand. "A man asked me to help him carry a case to the car park," he said. "But I told him I had to stay close to you."

"Good lad," said Grandpa. "Better safe than sorry."

"I felt a bit mean," Joe said. "He looked a nice man, and he really needed help."

Grandpa was still peering into oncoming headlights. "You still did the right thing," he said. "If he needs help, he'll find it. Don't you worry."

Joe bit his lip. "He won't think I'm rude?"

But Grandpa had spotted the car now, and he was busy waving it to a halt. So Nana answered.

"No," she said firmly. "He won't think you're rude. Good strangers always understand that you're just doing what you're told to do to stay safe. That's the good thing about safety rules. They make it easy to say no."

The car door was open now. As Nana clambered in, Joe thought about what she'd said. She was right. That *was* the good thing about safety rules. First they reminded you to stop and think and use your common sense. Then they made it easy to say no. And good strangers always understood.

"Good," he said. "*Good*." Just as he was about to climb into the car, a strong arm slid from nowhere around his waist, and hauled him back.

"What's good?" a gruff voice sounded in his ear. "The concert hall? The music? Or those very, very special third violins?"

Joe swung around. Stranger danger?

No. No one strange at all. Just his brother Tom in his dark suit and white bow tie, standing beside him clutching his violin case, and looking very, very proud.